Princess Bria
of Pickelot

Three Tales of Fantasy

DEDICATION

To my niece, Bria Laree Pickel, who helped inspire me to not only create the character of Princess Bria, but also to make an entire kingdom filled with magical adventures.

- Joe R. Frinzi, aka Sir Uncle Joe

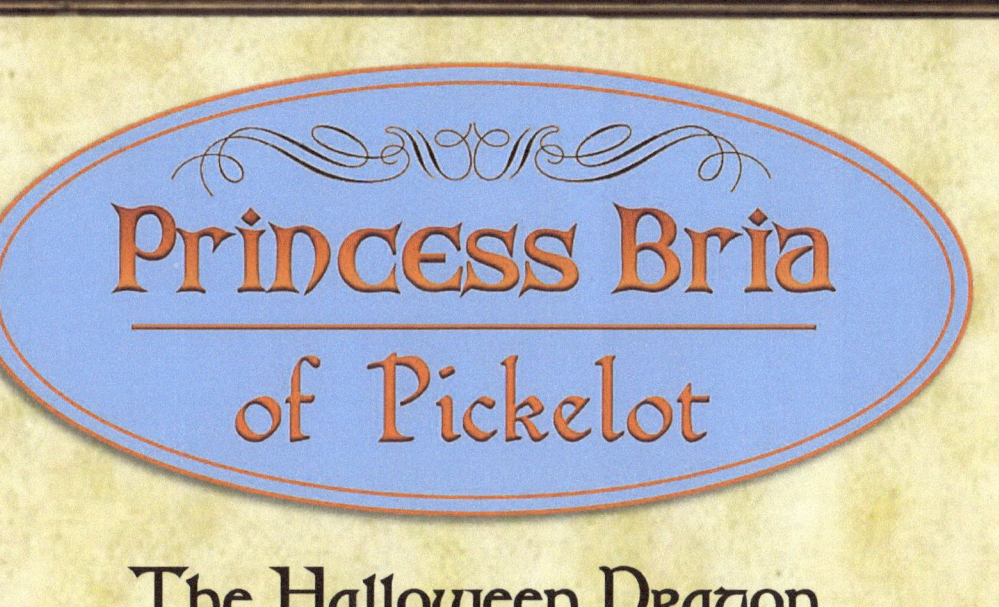

Princess Bria
of Pickelot

The Halloween Dragon

The Christmas Tree Forest

The Birthday Wish

Three tales of fantasy by
Joe R. Frinzi

Cover Art by
Cotty Kilbanks

"*Happy people make for a happy kingdom.*"

King Thomas

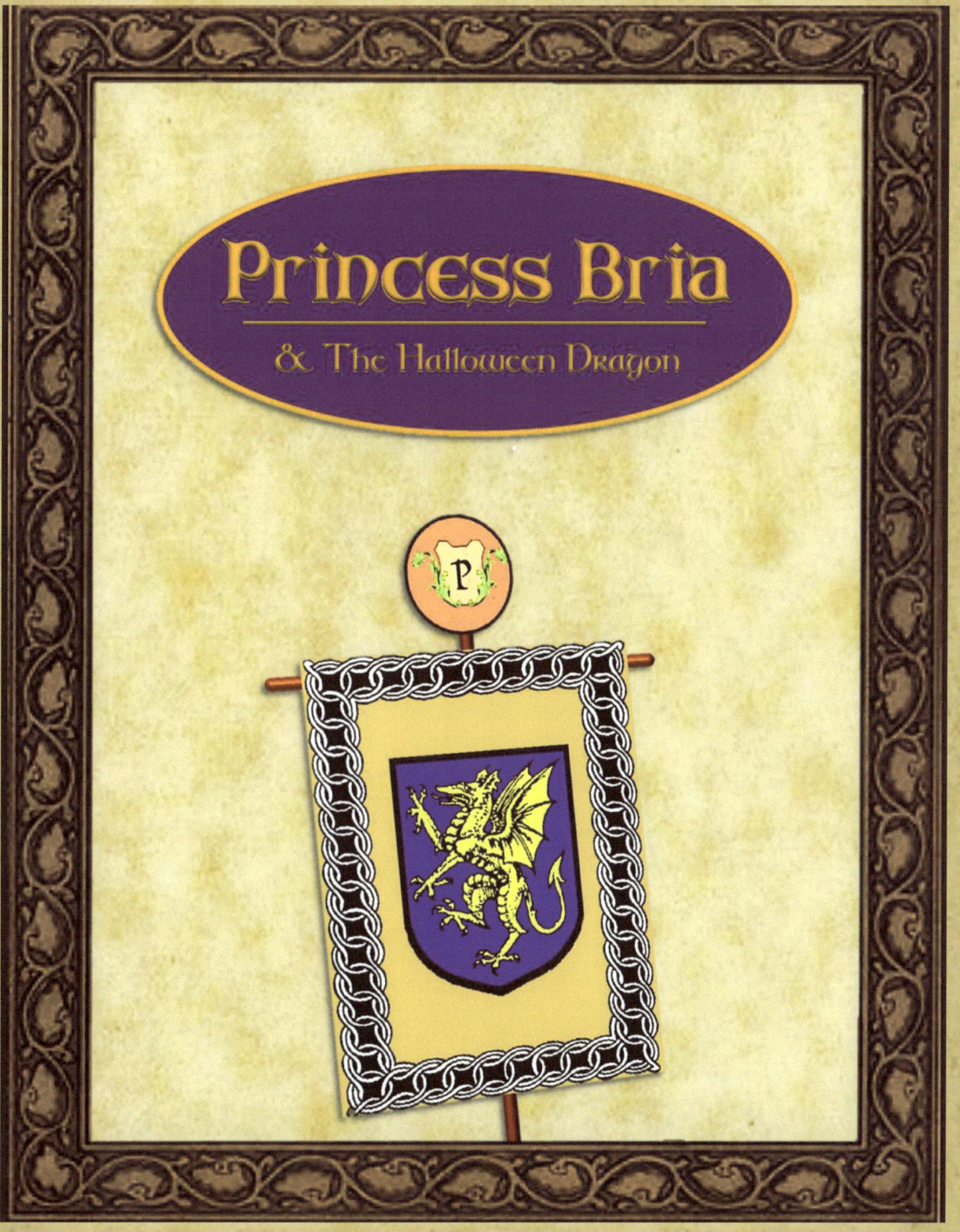

"Have no fear, my young Princess, I am here to protect you!"

Sir Joseph

PRINCESS BRIA
& THE HALLOWEEN DRAGON
By JOE R. FRINZI

Once upon a time in the magical kingdom of Pickelot, there lived a beautiful young Princess named Bria Laree. She loved to spend her time creating brightly colored dresses of delicate flowing fabrics, which she would then wear while telling pretend stories in which she was the main character. The Princess had a wonderful imagination and a big heart and she especially enjoyed playing with all the animals in her kingdom. Her parents, the King and Queen, loved Bria very much and raised her to be a kind, loving and generous young lady. She was equally loved and respected by everyone in the kingdom, from the servants and courtiers, to the maidens and the knights.

*

One knight in particular, her uncle, Sir Joseph, who she called Sir Uncle Joe, was especially fond of the young Princess and had vowed to be her protector. On a cold and rainy day in October Sir Joseph saw Princess Bria sitting alone in the great hall of the castle looking very sad. The knight approached her, bowed politely and with genuine concern asked, "What is it, young Princess, that makes you so sad?"

*

"Oh, Sir Uncle Joe," the girl replied with a heavy heart, "I wish to celebrate the Halloween holiday by dressing up in a lovely costume and giving out candy and other treats to my subjects, but I'm afraid my actions will bring forth the terrible Halloween Dragon."

*

The gallant knight looked perplexed. "What is this Halloween Dragon of which you speak?"

"He is a fearsome creature," said the Princess, her eyes growing wide with dread. "Whenever anyone tries to celebrate Halloween the monster may appear, letting loose ghosts and goblins from his fiery mouth, frightening everyone within sight."

"He sounds like a formidable beast," replied the knight, "but as your savior and protector, I pledge upon my honor to destroy this wretched brute which has caused you so much pain, so that you may celebrate the holiday as you desire."

"Oh, thank you, Sir Uncle Joe," said Bria with delight. "Now everyone in the kingdom will be able to enjoy Halloween without any fear."

"It is the least I can do for my favorite niece," replied the brave knight with a smile as he bowed respectfully and made his leave of the young girl.

*

The next day was bright and sunny as Princess Bria prepared for a festive Halloween celebration. She sent a decree that everyone was invited to dress up in their most colorful costumes and meet at the castle gate to receive candy and other special treats for the holiday. Hundreds of people showed up, from little children to adults, all attired in fantastical outfits of every color imaginable. The lovely Princess was there, too, in her most beautiful gown, bestowing treats to everyone. She looked absolutely radiant.

*

Just as the festivities were getting underway the sky turned dark and the horrid Halloween Dragon appeared, swooping down from the sky and landing near the castle. He was huge and fearsome, colored all black and purple with piercing red eyes that glowed like burning coals. Everyone was frightened by the sight of the menacing giant, especially Bria who cried out, "Oh no, why must this dreadful monster come here and destroy all our fun?" Fire and smoke surged from the great Dragon's snout, immediately becoming ghastly-looking ghosts and goblins and other nasty demons which flew and flitted about, terrifying all the people in the kingdom.

*

The Princess, herself, was terribly frightened and unable to even move, but then suddenly a loud booming voice behind her shouted out, "Have no fear, my young Princess, I am here to protect you." Bria looked over her shoulder and saw her uncle, Sir Joseph, wielding a large sword and riding forth from the castle on a great steed, both clad in full armor. "With my mighty sword," said the brave knight, "I will defeat this terrible beast and save the kingdom." As he approached the gigantic Dragon he raised his weapon which began to glow as if drawing power from some magical source. By now the ghosts and goblins were flying all around, making hideous cries and screams as they continued to pour out of the Dragon's flaming mouth.

*

Waving his glowing sword, a look of steely resolve on his face, Sir Joseph would not allow himself to be overwhelmed by his fear. "Away with you, you cursed Dragon!" he bellowed as a white-hot bolt of radiant energy flew from his sword. There was then a huge explosion as the ray of light struck the enormous body of the terrible beast, creating a black, smoky cloud which completely engulfed the Dragon and all the scary, flying creatures that surrounded it. The blast knocked the brave knight from his horse to the ground with a heavy thud. Smoke and dust were everywhere, making it difficult to see anything. The crowd was in a panic, now, as they tried to find their way amidst the noise and gloom of the billowing black clouds.

*

Unable to see her uncle, Bria ran out from the courtyard gate to make sure he was okay, quite forgetting her own fear for the moment. As the dust and smoke began to dissipate and clear, she arrived at the side of the fallen knight and was relieved to see that he was still alive.

*

"Are you alright, Sir Uncle Joe?" she asked in a trembling voice.

"I am unharmed, my Lady," replied Sir Joseph as he sat up and looked around. The smoky clouds had completely cleared by now and, as he rose to his feet, the brave knight made a startling discovery. Where the giant, fearsome Dragon had been, there was now only a tiny lizard, small enough to be held in one's hand. The innocent creature was perched on a rock, looking sheepishly about, and was obviously no danger to anyone. "Why, this little fellow isn't a threat to any of us," said Sir Joseph as he gazed upon the harmless animal.

*

"Why was he so fearsome, before?" asked Bria, clearly bewildered by this change of events.

"I don't think he ever really was," said the knight, slowly putting all the facts together in his mind. "I think we only *thought* he was fearsome, because we were so afraid. Our imaginations and our fears are what made him seem real." Sir Joseph turned to the Princess and, though he had always loved her, he suddenly now had an even greater respect for his young niece. "But when I fought the Dragon and you thought I was hurt," he continued, "you put aside your own fears and came to my aid. So you see, when you are brave such fears can do you no harm. And that's what this Dragon always was, just a made up fear in our imaginations."

*

The Princess and her uncle looked down at the little lizard who then jumped off the rock and scampered away. Bria gave a soft giggle and said, "He's actually quite a cute little creature, isn't he? How could I ever have been afraid of him?"

"Indeed," replied Sir Joseph, "he's certainly no danger to any of us. It was our fear which made him seem a menace."

"Yes," said the newly wise Princess, "that must be the answer. I will therefore never allow my fears to take control of my life again."

*

Well, with the imaginary Dragon gone for good, the people of Pickelot returned to enjoy their celebration. They wore their colorful costumes and danced and feasted and everyone received candy, all courtesy of the generous young Princess. At the end of the day, the King and Queen announced that this was the most joyous celebration the kingdom had ever held.

*

When Princess Bria went to bed that night she knew that everything was safe and secure in her world. She thought about her brave uncle, Sir Joseph, and realized that if she were ever frightened again, she could draw upon that same courage within herself. And, just like that, all the fears she ever had were gone. There would be many more Halloween celebrations to come, and Princess Bria knew that she would never be afraid again.

*

THE END

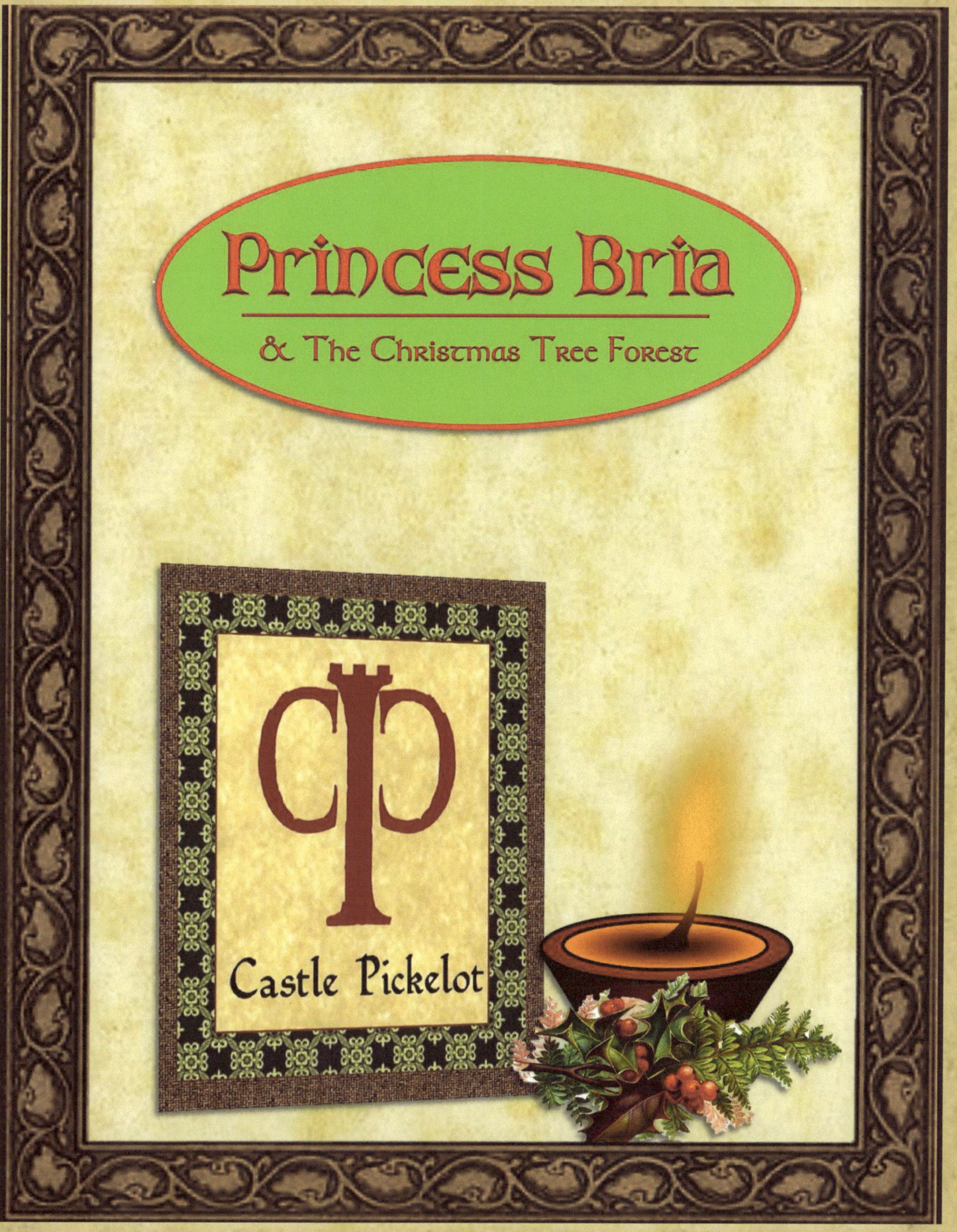

"*Now I will be able to give the kingdom the best Christmas present ever!*"

Princess Bria

PRINCESS BRIA
& THE CHRISTMAS TREE FOREST
BY JOE R. FRINZI

Once upon a time in the magical kingdom of Pickelot, there lived a beautiful young Princess named Bria Laree. She had a very generous nature and was well loved by everyone in the kingdom. She would spend her days making wonderful gifts for her family and friends, as well as for all of her subjects, and greatly enjoyed giving them out during the holidays and other special occasions. While any occasion would do, she was especially fond of Christmas time.

*

As the Yuletide holiday approached, the young Princess began thinking very hard about what she might do for everyone in the kingdom this particular season. In years past she had made wreaths and candles and even colorful scarves and hats, but this year she knew she needed to do something extra special. One evening in the dining hall she spoke with her parents, the King and Queen, about what she should do that coming Christmas. The wise Royal couple offered her their advice:

"We have always done what we could for our subjects," said King Thomas, "since happy people make for a happy kingdom. What you choose to do can only be determined by yourself if it is to be sincere."

Queen Stephanie agreed and had this to add. "You must look within your heart for the answer. Every year you face this challenge and every year you make the right choice. I trust you shall do so again."

"Thank you, mother and father," replied Bria, "I know I must find this answer within myself, and I'm sure I shall." The young Princess then headed off to her room to think on the matter.

*

Alone in her bedroom, Bria sat and wondered over what she should do. She thought about all the ways she had tried to make Christmas a festive holiday. For as long as she could remember it had been treated as a quiet and solemn occasion. She had done her best to bring color and joy each time with her scarves, hats and wreaths, but she wanted to do something this year that could be enjoyed by the entire kingdom.

Looking out her window from high in the castle, Bria could see the great evergreen forest spread out just beyond the village. It was a dark and mysterious mass in the night, barely seen under the half-lit moon. Bria recalled that on those rare occasions when snow fell on Pickelot, it would cling to the treetops, making the forest much more visible, even when there was no moon out to light the land.

*

As she looked on, the forest suddenly and unexpectedly began to shimmer in the pale moonlight, which made Bria gasp aloud. She had noticed this effect before, which was caused by ice on the trees! A brief storm must have passed by the forest, she thought, covering the trees with ice. At once, Bria knew what she would do this Christmas. She had her answer and would begin her plans in the morning.

*

The next day, after breakfast, Bria went to the stables to see her uncle, Sir Joseph, who she always addressed as Sir Uncle Joe.

"Greetings, fair Princess," said Sir Joseph when the girl arrived at the stables. "What can I do for my favorite niece?"

"Greetings to you, Sir Uncle Joe," replied the Princess. "I have decided what I want to do this Christmas holiday, but will require your help to accomplish it."

"You need only ask and it is yours," said the brave knight.

"Well," laughed Bria, "you may regret making such an offer when you hear what I need. I would like you to find the finest large tree in the evergreen forest and bring it back whole to the castle!"

"Indeed," said Sir Joseph. "That is a challenge worthy of a knight! I heartily accept your request since I know it must come from some good place in your soul."

"Thank you, Sir Uncle Joe," the girl said, clasping her hands with delight. "Now I will be able to give the kingdom the best Christmas present ever!"

*

Sir Joseph immediately gathered together a number of stable hands to obtain a wooden cart, strong enough to hold a giant tree. They then rode out to the evergreen forest beyond the village. Once there, they soon determined which tree would best suit the Princess's need and quickly brought it down with a great, thundering crash. Under the knight's instruction the men loaded the gigantic tree, roots and all, onto the horse-drawn cart and returned it to the castle where the Princess was waiting for them by the entrance. Everyone wondered just what she was up to, but all she would say was that it was going to be a surprise.

*

For the next week Bria worked in secret in the Great Hall of the castle. No one was allowed to enter, except for a small group of villagers who had volunteered their services for the Princess's mysterious project. Not even the King and Queen were allowed in, much to their amusement, as it appeared their own daughter had become the new temporary leader of Pickelot!

*

Finally, the young Princess announced that she was ready to unveil her Christmas gift to the kingdom. A decree was issued that everyone was invited to visit the castle to see the special gift the Princess had created. The people began arriving almost at once and soon a huge crowd appeared at the castle gate. Before they were allowed to enter, however, the King and Queen and Sir Joseph were given a private viewing.

*

When they entered the Great Hall they couldn't believe their eyes. Everywhere, the entire room had been decorated with holly and wreaths, candles and ribbons. It was the most spectacular display they had ever seen. And at the center of the Hall, the giant evergreen tree that Sir Joseph had acquired for the Princess, stood tall and proud and was equally adorned with all manner of decoration, from colored pine cones to golden rope encircling its enormous size. Hundreds of lit candles in special holders were on the branches creating a shimmering effect unlike anything ever seen before.

*

"My Princess, you have truly created a miracle," said Sir Joseph, totally in awe of what he was seeing. "How on earth did you ever think of such a thing as this?"

"The night before I asked you to bring me the tree," said Bria, "I saw the forest covered in ice from my bedroom window. It shimmered in the moonlight and that is when the idea came to me."

"I recall that evening," said Sir Joseph, somewhat perplexed. "I was in the forest that night and I can assure you there was no ice. In fact, it was rather warm for the season." The knight then turned to his young niece and said, "We do not get snow very often, here in Pickelot, so I believe there must have been some higher force at work to inspire you that night."

*

"Perhaps you are right," replied the Princess as she thought about what her uncle said. "Though I have given this gift of a decorated tree to my subjects, by some means it first had to be given to me."

"Yes," said Queen Stephanie, "this is truly a Divine gift."

*

The villagers were then welcomed inside the Great Hall to look upon the wonderful gift from their Princess. The King and Queen handed out presents, the minstrels played songs and everyone enjoyed fine food and drink. Sir Joseph and Bria sat off to one side and gazed out the window, savoring the joyfulness of the newly festive holiday. The nearly full moon cast its rays brightly across the land as peace reigned over the kingdom. And then, very quietly, tiny flakes of snow began to fall.

*

That Christmas Eve in Pickelot was the best that anyone in the kingdom could remember. Bria never felt closer or happier with her family and friends than she did that night. The holiday, which had always been observed in a cold and solemn manner, would be celebrated, from now on, as festive and warm. Everyone was grateful for the wonderful gift their young Princess had bestowed upon them, and she, in turn understood that the joy they were feeling was their gift to her. There would be many more Christmas celebrations to come, and Princess Bria knew that the spirit of giving would always be alive in her heart.

*

THE END

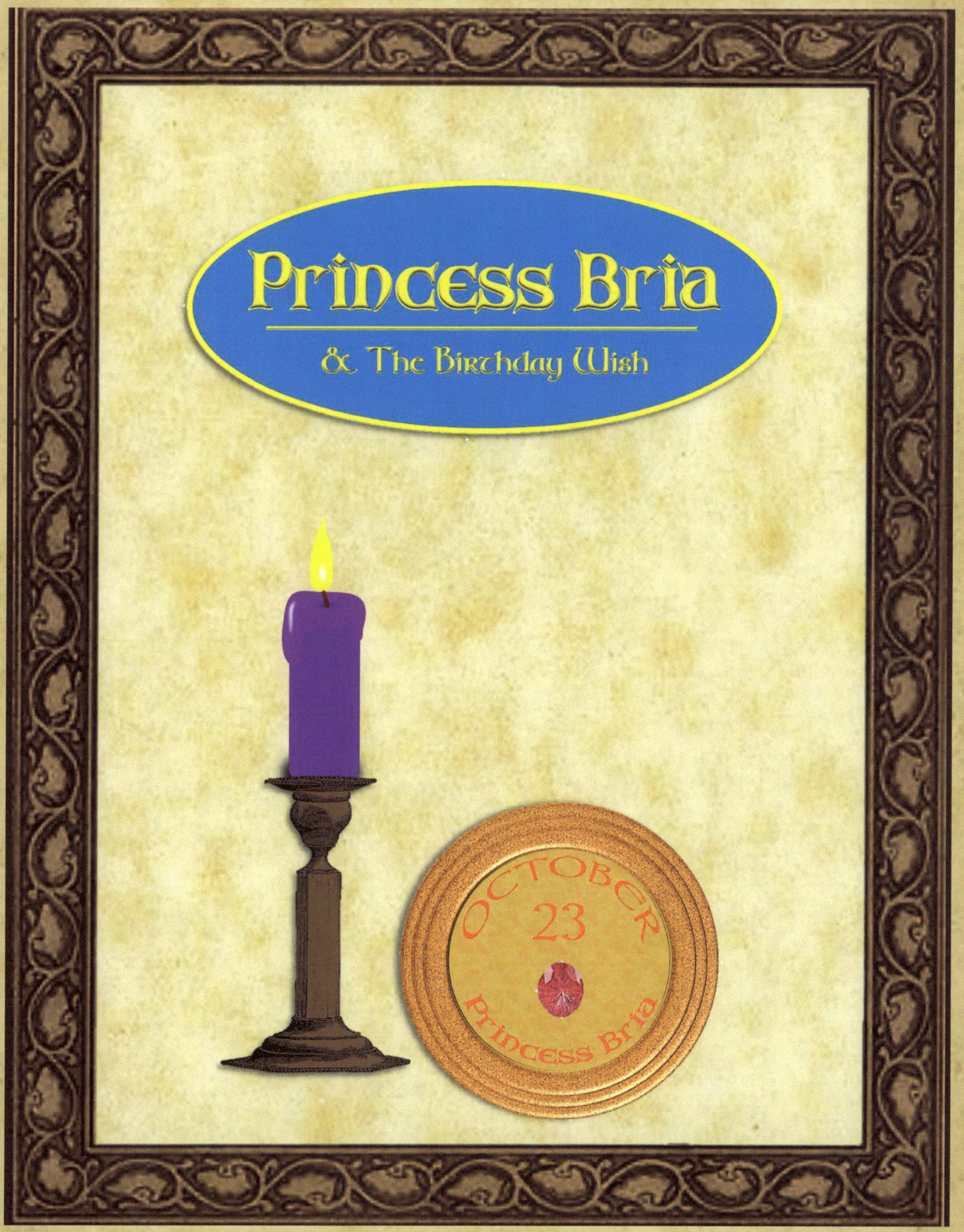

"*Being a mother myself, I know that a parent's love knows no bounds.*"

Queen Stephanie

PRINCESS BRIA
& THE BIRTHDAY WISH
BY JOE R. FRINZI

Once upon a time in the magical kingdom of Pickelot, there lived a beautiful young Princess named Bria Laree. She was a kind and generous little girl, and often came up with ways to bring happiness to others. One of her favorite methods for doing this was to hold elaborate birthday parties for the other children in the village. One day she had the idea to visit the orphanage where children lived who had no parents. When she met with the people who worked there, Bria learned that the twelve young orphans who were there had never had a birthday party because they didn't know the date when they were born. The young Princess immediately decided to give them the best birthday party ever.

*

Upon meeting the children, Princess Bria asked them what sort of party they would like to have. Even though they were surprised that a royal Princess would want to meet with them, the orphans quickly realized how warm and sincere she was, and offered up their ideas for a party that included cake and other treats, entertaining games to play and a present they could each call their own. When Bria asked what sort of gift they would like, one of the children pointed to the Princess's birthstone pendant, which had the month and day inscribed on it, and replied that the best present they could ever receive was to know the date of their real birthday. All the children agreed that this is what they truly wanted.

*

In speaking with the orphanage caretakers, Bria was told that no records existed for the birthdates of the orphans. In many cases, the children had been infants when they arrived at the orphanage and there was no way to tell exactly when they were born. Since there were twelve children at the orphanage, Bria decided to have special birthstone pendants, just like her own, made for each one of them as a surprise present, covering the twelve months of the year. Even though the actual birthdates were unknown, the pendants would still be a keepsake the children could call their own.

*

Bria then made her way to the village jeweler and asked her to create twelve new pendants, exactly like her own, each one with a different birthstone. When the jeweler asked what dates she wanted inscribed, the Princess said that since no actual birthdates were known, just the individual months would have to do.

*

Back at the castle Bria began planning the special birthday celebration for the orphans. The King and Queen both agreed to help out with decorating the Great Hall, as well as making the treats. Even Bria's uncle, Sir Joseph, who she always called Sir Uncle Joe, said he would try to find out more information about the orphans and perhaps learn their actual birthdates. "Thank you, Sir Uncle Joe," said the grateful Princess, "I'm sure my new friends would be so pleased to know their real birthdays."

"Not at all, my lovely niece," replied the gallant knight. "It is always an honor to serve you."

*

On the day of the party the orphans excitedly arrived at the castle and were overwhelmed by all the decorations that had been put up. They'd never seen anything like it before. Tables laden with cakes and snacks were everywhere, while a band of musicians played spirited music and court jesters provided lively entertainment. The Princess herself, though happy to greet all the children, was a bit distracted since the gift pendants had yet to be delivered.

*

It wasn't until the party had been going on for some time that the jeweler finally arrived at the castle with the pendants. The young Princess was relieved to see her and asked what had caused the delay. The jeweler apologized and said that it took longer to finish the work than she had expected. Bria quickly took the wrapped packages and began distributing them to the excited children who had eagerly gathered around her.

*

Once all the wrapped gifts had been handed out, Princess Bria held up her own pendant and made an announcement. "To all my new friends from the orphanage, each of you has been given a very special present from all of us here at Castle Pickelot. Even though we do not know your exact birthdates, I had the village jeweler make you a birthstone pendant like the one I have. Since there are twelve of you, she made one for each month of the year, so you would each have a unique gift to call your own."

*

The children then eagerly opened their gifts and gazed lovingly at their very own birthstone pendants. They were made of bronze with the individual month inscribed, and had a colorful birthstone gem set in the center. Almost immediately, however, the children discovered that along with the month and their name, each pendant also carried a specific date, something that was impossible for anyone to know.

*

The startled Princess turned to the jeweler and asked her how this could be. The jeweler replied that a mysterious courier had visited her shop the day before and delivered a message that contained all the birthdate information necessary to make the pendants truly accurate, which is why she was so late in delivering the gifts. Bria immediately turned to her uncle and said "I'm sure this could only have been due to your hard work, Sir Uncle Joe. You said you would find out the birthdates of the orphans and you did! Thank you so much."

"It was not I, my Lady," said the mystified knight. "It's true I tried to find out the information you sought, but I could learn nothing, despite my efforts."

*

At this point Bria's mother, Queen Stephanie, stepped forward. "My dear daughter Bria," said the wise Queen, "I think I may have the answer. Being a mother myself, I know that a parent's love knows no bounds. I believe that the spirits of the departed parents somehow brought this information to the jeweler so that the pendants could be properly made and that their children would know just how much they are loved."

The jeweler nodded her head in agreement. "All I know is that the courier who delivered the birth information to me was like no other I'd ever seen before. He very well might have been a messenger from beyond this world."

*

Bria looked at the happy, shining faces of all the orphans whose eyes were glistening with delight as they held their pendants tightly in their small hands. Deep inside she realized that the joy they felt in knowing their birthday came from a place far more important than the simple gesture she had made of giving them the pendants. Though she'd always been well-loved herself, at that moment Bria understood fully what it meant to feel the love of a parent and what a special gift that truly is.

*

The party continued well into the evening and when the children were finally escorted home, each one thanked the young Princess for helping them discover their own special birthday. Bria also promised them each another party at Castle Pickelot on their actual birthday. As such, there would be many more birthday celebrations to come, and

Princess Bria knew that each and every one would be a special gift of love in its own right.

*

THE END

Castle Pickelot

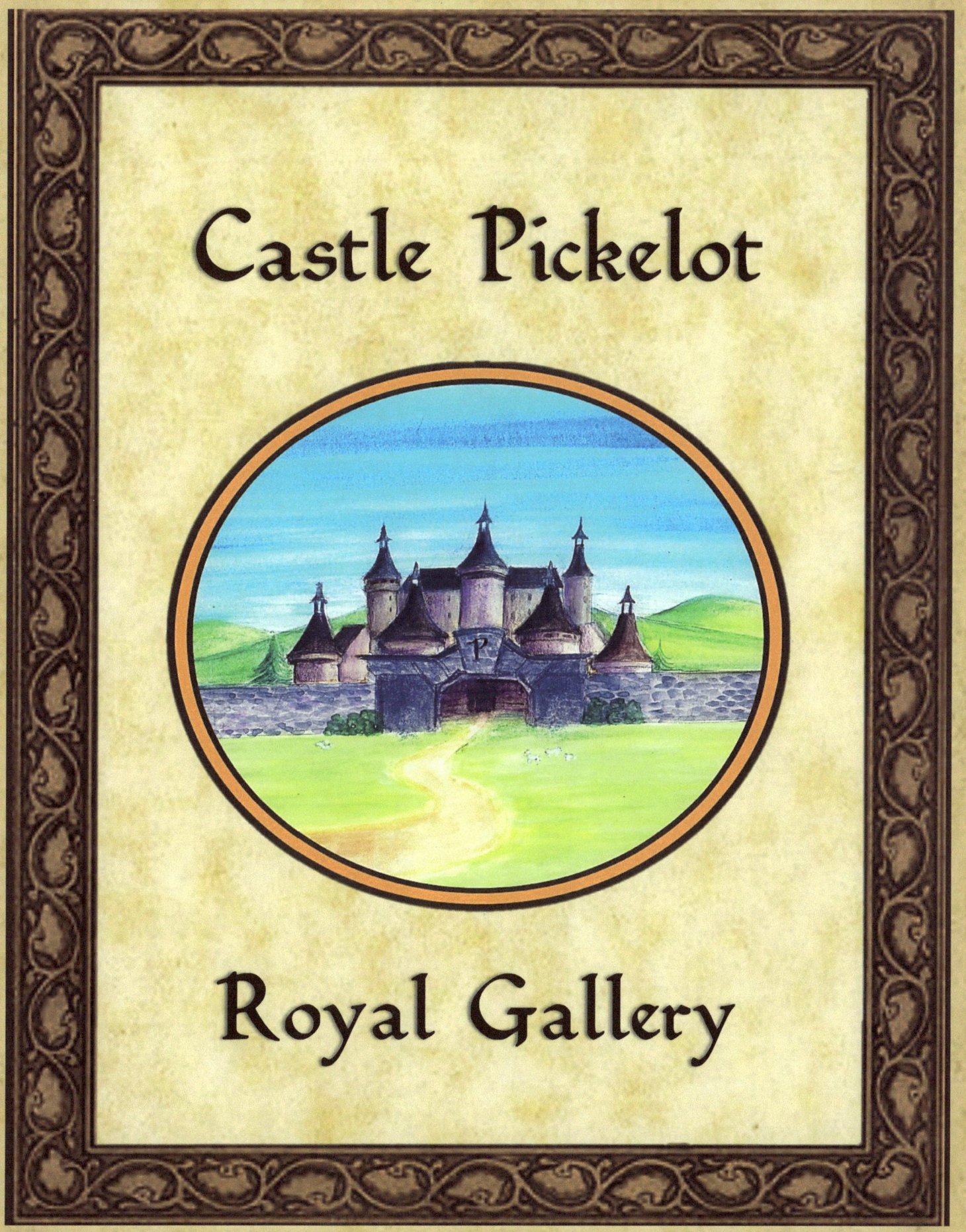

Royal Gallery

Royal Gallery One

Pickelot Kingdom Shield Emblem

Castle Pickelot Banner

Knights of Pickelot Banner

Royal Gallery Two

Princess Bria Banner

Sir Joseph
Dragon Standard

Queen Stephanie Banner

King Thomas Banner

All Are

Kingdom of Pickelot

Welcome